For Mum, Dad, Siobhan, Dan, and Tristan—for those hours spent in shoe shops.
And for Elaine—who wasn't family but did it out of friendship!
L.S.

For Bea x
D.T.

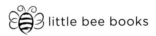 little bee books
A division of Bonnier Publishing
853 Broadway, New York, New York 10003
Text copyright © 2016 by Leilani Sparrow
Illustrations copyright © 2016 by Dan Taylor
First published in Great Britain by Boxer Books Limited.
This little bee books edition, 2016.
Manufactured in China TOPPAN 0416
First Edition
2 4 6 8 10 9 7 5 3 1
Library of Congress Cataloging-in-Publication Data is available upon request.
ISBN 978-1-4998-0363-1
littlebeebooks.com
bonnierpublishing.com

My New Shoes

by Leilani Sparrow
illustrated by Dan Taylor

little bee books

My feet are growing.
What great news!

It's time to buy
a pair of shoes.

Dad and I are on the train.

I'm wearing nice
clean socks again.

In the shoe store,
find a chair.

I see feet,
feet, everywhere!

We need to find
the perfect fit.

Let's measure them.
You've grown a bit.

**Maybe you need
shoes for school.**

Shoes with heels
would be so cool.

Do I need rain boots for the rain?

Sandals for sun . . . or sneakers for games?

Shoes that look
like scary sharks . . .

or shoes that light
up in the dark?

How about shoes
with bows that tie?

So many shoes!
Oh, what to buy?

All new shoes
are shiny and neat.

I want new shoes
that fit my feet.

Look, we have them. Try this pair.

Walk around from here to there.

Do they pinch?
No, not a bit.

Hooray, you have
new shoes that fit!

You can walk or you
can run. . . .

New shoes can
be so much fun!

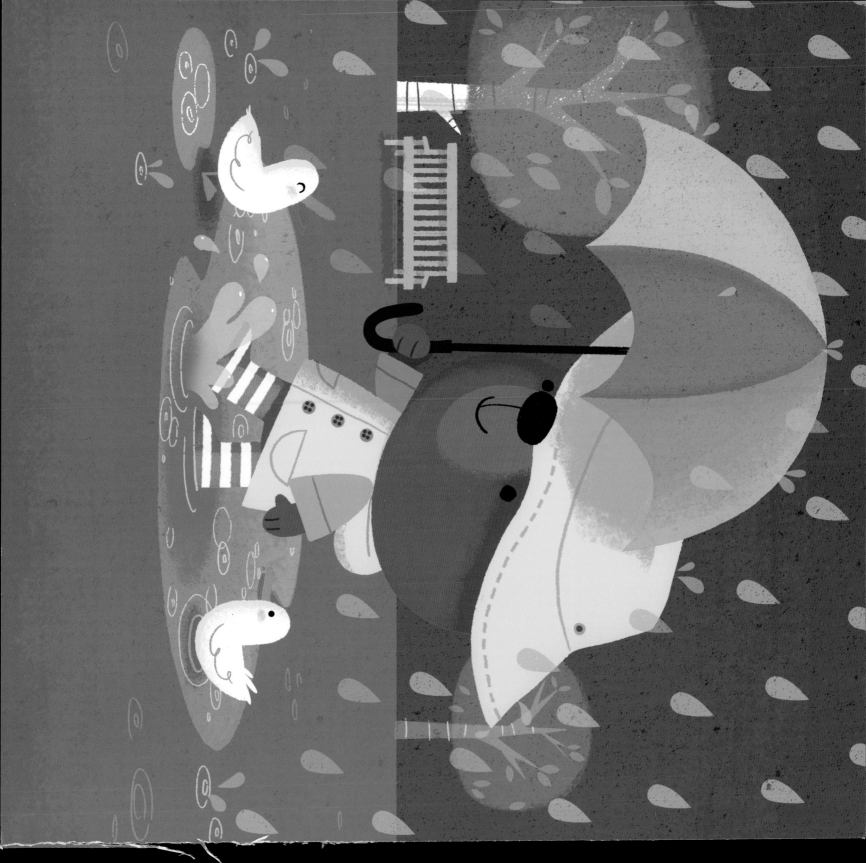